The Parrot Family

By

Frank S. Anthony

Cover artwork - Jorge Pacheco

ISBN 978-0-473-55423-1

The Parrot Family
Author Frank S. Anthony
Published by AG Books
Whanganui
New Zealand

Foreword

Frank Sheldon Anthony

A distinctively New Zealand writer

It takes a skilled writer to capture the feel of a culture. As Murray Ball would for a later generation, Frank Sheldon Anthony did for his. He captured the vicissitudes, and most importantly the humour, of life as a farmer in the 'back blocks'. Like Ball, he didn't just write about this life, he lived it. His *Me and Gus* stories showed farm life as it really was in the Taranaki, reflected through the dry wit of the kiwi farmer.

Frank Sheldon Anthony was born on 13 December 1891 at Matawhero, near Gisborne. His father, also Frank Sheldon Anthony, never really settled into any one career. At various times he ran a hotel, owned racehorses, farmed, and finally settled in the remote settlement of Whakamara. It was here that Frank Junior's mother, Annie, taught the local one-teacher school. All of Frank's three sisters would later become schoolteachers as well. Both Frank Senior (who died in 1935) and Annie (who died in 1953) are buried in Patea Cemetery in South Taranaki.

Frank Sheldon Anthony junior grew up in Taranaki. He finished his primary education at Whakamara School, most likely as a student of his mother, who strongly encouraged his writing. From about the age of ten, he began to fill exercise books with stories of the events around him, a habit he would maintain in various forms for the rest of his life. After his primary schooling, he spent two years at Hāwera District High School, before starting work as a farmhand. The teenaged Anthony, though, was not ready to settle into a farming life in the 'back of beyond'.

In 1909, while on holiday in Auckland, Anthony went to sea, working initially as a deckhand on New Zealand coastal steamers. This was not enough for the adventurous young man, though. Soon, he joined the sailors aboard the merchant sailing vessels that still dominated international trade in the early twentieth century. For the next few years, Anthony explored the world aboard the windjammers, travelling to Asia, Europe, and the Americas. Luckily for his family, he remained an avid writer and would keep them updated on his journeys.

Like so many of his countrymen, Anthony responded rapidly to the outbreak of World War One. At twenty-three years old, he left his ship in San Francisco and travelled to England to join the Royal Navy. Anthony was posted to the destroyer *Opal* and served in the North Atlantic. The *Opal* was among the British ships engaged in the Battle at Jutland. Anthony's letters to his mother describe, in vivid detail, the experience of living through the war's largest naval battle.

Shortly after Jutland, Anthony was seriously injured when he was crushed between his ship and a buoy. The accident severely damaged his lungs and resulted in an extended hospital stay. In 1918, he was invalided back to New Zealand, where he spent several months in the Te Waikato Sanatorium at Cambridge. The injury would plague him for the rest of his life, leading to pneumonia and a general weakness of the lungs.

In 1919 Anthony was considered well enough to be discharged. Though he had a naval pension, it was not really enough to constitute a living income. Anthony decided to return to the farming life. Using a soldiers' rehabilitation grant he purchased a 76-acre (30-hectare) dairy farm on Denbigh Road, near Midhirst, in the shadow of Mount Taranaki. For nearly five years he struggled with ill health and a farm that was cold, swampy, and in need of a great deal of work. He sold up in 1924 to move to England.

It was while farming in Taranaki that Anthony first achieved success as a writer. A bachelor, isolated on his remote farm, he filled his evenings writing. Between 1923 and 1924 two of his novels, *Follow The Call* and *Windjammer Sailors*, were published in Christchurch's *The Weekly Press.* It was at this time too that he took incidents from the rural world around him and began writing them into humorous stories. These were made into ten *Me and Gus* stories about the misadventures of two bachelor farmers in the Taranaki that were published in both *The Weekly Press* and *Auckland Weekly News.*

Following his success in New Zealand, Anthony once again decided farming was not for him. In 1924 he moved to England, intending to continue his writing career, and in pursuit of a young Taranaki woman he hoped to marry. In both cases, he was to be disappointed. There was no marriage, and he was unable to break into the English writing market, despite toning down the Kiwi idiom in the *Me and Gus* stories. He wrote more short fiction, and further pieces based on his seagoing experiences, but to little avail.

The climate of England did not suit Anthony's health. Tuberculosis, exacerbated by his lung damage, began to take its toll, and by 1926 he was clearly in decline. On 13 January, 1927, Frank Sheldon

Anthony—writer, farmer, and war veteran—died in a boarding house at Boscombe, near Bournemouth. He was buried in England, half a world away from the Taranaki he had so eloquently brought to life.

It is clear that Anthony loved writing, and had a remarkable ability to express his world vividly on paper. From an early age, he spent much of his spare time writing, filling books with stories and descriptions of life around him, as well as writing voluminous letters about his experiences sailing around the world. The National Library of New Zealand holds an extensive collection of his earlier writings, covering a vast range of subjects, and fictional genres.

It is Anthony's *Gus and Me* stories that he is best known for. Written during his time farming in Taranaki they capture the spirit of the time and place. These stories are written in the vernacular of the world he inhabited, a masculine world of hardworking cow-cockies dealing with poor-quality land, debt, and an uncertain financial future. While the stories include the gentle humour and dry wit typical of New Zealand, they also offer a strong social commentary, pointing out that New Zealand in the 1920s was not really the land of equality and opportunity that the myth of the day made it out to be. As both comic stories of romantic and farming misadventure, and as a window on life in the Taranaki at the time, they remain classic examples of New Zealand literature.

Two of his novels, *Follow the Call* and *Gus Tomlins*, are set in the same environment. *Follow the Call* is a romantic comedy loosely based on Anthony's own experiences, with a similar feel to the *Gus and Me* stories. *Gus Tomlins*, which was never published during Anthony's life, is a novel based on the same stories.

Windjammer Sailors, on the other hand, is an exciting tale of life aboard the sailing ships that crossed the Pacific before World War One. In *Windjammer Sailors* Anthony makes it clear, despite the romance at the end of the age of sail, that life aboard these vessels could be tough. He did not shy from dealing with the social realities of his day, either aboard ship or in Taranaki.

None of Anthony's works were published in book form during his lifetime. In fact, while the *Gus and Me* serials were well received, it is really only after his death that he developed much of a public following. His mother arranged for the publication of *Follow the Call* in 1936. More importantly, she passed Anthony's *Me and Gus* manuscripts to Francis Jackson in the 1950s. He rewrote them for radio, bringing the stories to a much wider audience in New Zealand. It was to be the mid-1970s, though, before Auckland University Press published *Gus Tomlins*.

Frank Sheldon Anthony remains an important, if little recognised today, figure in New Zealand writing. He is among the earliest writers in New Zealand to really capture the local culture, in its language and dry humour. In the early part of the twentieth century, most material that New Zealanders read came from abroad, mostly England. Anthony, instead, wrote about New Zealand, for New Zealanders, in a New Zealand voice. For this, if for nothing else, he deserves greater recognition.

This story, The Parrot Family, is a previously unpublished example of Anthony's earlier writing. It is believed to have been written in 1903, before Anthony ever left New Zealand. While it may lack the polish of some of his later work, it is well written given the author's age at the time. The language may be a little dated, looking back more to the nineteenth century than the twentieth, but it does show Anthony's eye for the environment around him. The story, despite some 'English' touches, is very certainly set in New Zealand—somewhere near Hāwera in fact. Here, then, is the Taranaki of over a century ago, as seen by a young man, just mastering his writing craft.

– D B Hann, September 2020

A note on editing: The text has been transcribed from the original handwritten document and edited only for consistency, spelling and grammar, for ease of reading.

Chapter 1

One bleak, cold morning a battered, mud-splashed old gig, drawn by a worn-out draft horse, might have been seen slowly winding its way down the busy streets of the busy town of Hāwera. The occupants of this battered vehicle were two boys of 12 years, and an old grey-bearded man of 70. The old man seemed intent on driving, while the boys—who sat by his side—were occupied in looking carefully at each shop they passed.

Anon, they glanced impatiently at some bright new carriage as it dashed swiftly by, or a gaudy, green bicycle, or a small red one, propelled by a boy of eight, would attract their attention.

This dull cargo of boys and the old man were the Parrot family. James Marmaduke Parrot and William Albert Parrot—boys of spirit to be sure, and boys who well-merited their high names, as we shall see. Old Mr Parrot was their grandpapa. He was taking them to the annual show of the great city, and under the seat whereon they sat, there reposed the finest calf man ever saw. It was to win the first prize of £5, so Grandpa said, and so the boys believed. Did not Grandpa always know what he was talking about, and did not every word he said always come true?

We shall not go into details concerning the great show; suffice it to say that James Marmaduke and William Albert were disappointed in their expectations. They showered numerous hard names on the unconscious author of their disappointments—namely, the red- faced, potty old gentleman who had judged the department of prize calves, and went off to find Grandpa, whom they were firmly convinced would denounce the poor judge to his face. Grandpa fell greatly in their esteem, when he declined to execute their wishes, and consequently the red-faced judge went home that night under the impression that he had judged excellently, and pleased everybody. A sad mistake for a man of the world to make, for as we know, it is utterly impossible to please everybody. However, Grandpa denounced the judge quite enough to the boys on the way home to please them, and so, to tell the truth, did many another honest farmer disappointed in his expectations.

Old Parrot House, as it was called, was a fine, large mansion, considerably battered and oldish, however—as was everything else around—and largely in want of window frames. Around the large, black door there clung a thick arch of ivy, and the same creeper covered one side of the house, and enveloped the large veranda in a green mantle.

The house was surrounded by a thick barberry hedge, which same also enclosed a fairly large orchard, on which little green apples grew in clusters. Outside the hedge was a small paddock that contained a trap shed, a barn, and a cow shed. In the barn was a loft, where the two boys often played, and which was always full of straw. The old gentleman kept a cow, which the boys had to milk, and great were the quarrels caused thereby; for, should they ever go anywhere, one of them had always to return to milk the cow. As they both objected to milking in turns, this, as I have said, often caused serious quarrels. A quarrel over one cow, when every boy of their acquaintance milked at least 10.

Chapter 2

James Marmaduke and William Albert Parrot were twins and, if a fine name helps one any in this world, the reader will easily see that they had every chance of a prosperous life.

Their father, William Parrot, was killed in 1896, by a railway accident, and two years later saw their mother dead, also. The boys thus fell into their grandfather's hands, and, he being a rich, careless old gentleman, they had every luxury they wished for, and soon fell into the old man's mode of living.

Both attended the little school boasted by the Waverley township, and it is there, after breakfast, that we intend to accompany them. The room, honoured by the presence of the twins at night-time, was a large, lonely apartment, with a considerable lack of furniture and two handsome, oak-nailed beds of strong manufacture, leaning against the wall.

Mr Parrot kept two servants: an old man, John, and a girl, Polly. Polly cooked the food and did the more genteel work, while John scrubbed floors, cleaned knives, and did all outdoor work except milk the cow.

Half past seven. John always wakes the boys at this hour, so he trudged into their room as usual and shouted and pushed at them. How soundly they slept, with their heads under the blankets. Suddenly a bright idea occurred to John. He winked to himself and went out. Presently he returned with a mug of water which he carefully poured onto each boy's head. Poor John nearly got his dismissal for that little joke, and it was from regard of his past services that he was kept.

After breakfast—porridge, which the boys didn't like, but in default of something better, ate—William milked the cow, and then off they started for the school. They were not hailed very enthusiastically at school (but they did not notice) and, after William had hurt about three little boys, and James a corresponding number (just for fun), they ventured on a game of marbles. When James had lost all his marbles he stood up and accused his rival of cheating.

"I didn't!" started the lad, hotly. "I'm not a sneak, like you, Jim Parrot."

"All right, call me a sneak, will you?" said Mr James Marmaduke, tossing his head, and walked into school.

Presently the bell rang and the scholars marched into school. There was going to be a row, all the pupils agreed to that. The girls were one and all delighted, as is the custom of girls, and the boys were some glad, some sorry. Their teacher, a broad, stern-faced man approaching fifty, had all the boys drawn up in line in front of him.

"Now, James Parrot," said he, bringing his cane a rap on a desk that made everyone start. "Did Richard Sharpe cheat you at marbles, or no? That's cheating," the good man added. "Look me straight in the face and answer."

"Yes sir," answered James, doing as he was told, but in a blinking kind of way. "Please sir, William saw him, too."

"Did you see this boy cheat at marbles, William?" the teacher asked.

"Yes sir," answered William, blushing and eyeing his boots as he spoke.

"Very well, then," said the master. "Did you cheat this boy at marbles, Richard?" he continued.

"No, sir," said Richard, looking his questioner straight in the face.

Poor Dickie Sharpe; he had only his word to give against the other two, and the master was against him. Not only was he deprived of the marbles, but he got a sound thrashing as well.

"I abhor dishonesty in any form," said the old school master, as he sent Dickie to his seat. "And if any of you boys try it at this school, I'll serve you the same."

Had any of the gentle readers of this book been in the master's place at school, they could not but have noticed a boy of 10 years sitting at his desk trying to do a sum. But every five minutes his hand would brush his eyes, and he would find that the slate was wet with tears, and his sum all smudged and blotched. Poor Dickie. It was not the thrashing, it was the injustice, and at times you might have noticed his teeth set and his hand clench. At such a time Dickie (age10) was thinking of the punching he was going to give James (age 12), when he got the chance. After school, Master Dickie Sharpe wended his way homewards. But he said nothing to his father of the injustice done to him by his teacher, while on the other hand, Master James bragged in a stupendous manner of the occurrence to his grandpapa.

Mr and Mrs Sharpe had three children—two small girls and Dickie—and milked 30 cows, by which they earned their living. Of these Dickie milked 12 himself, his father about 14, and Mrs Sharpe the rest. There was much difference in these three boys, William and James, and Dickie. The two larger boys who lived in luxury, and Dickie, who had to get up before daylight and milk his 12 cows before he came to school.

Mr Sharpe was not a hard man. It was pure necessity that made him treat Dickie as he did. If Dickie didn't milk, he'd have to pay a man to, and he couldn't afford it. Anyway, it was good training for the boy. Teach him to be hardy. Didn't he get his sixpence a month to spend as he pleased? Some boys never get anything but blows for their work. And anyway, didn't all the other boys have to milk? Yes, one man beats a horse to death. Do all the other men say, "He did it, why shouldn't I?" And accordingly beat their horses too? I fancy not. But of course, cases are different.

Dickie's sisters were Tillie and Nell. Two bright eyed little maids, who seldom quarrelled and never for over five minutes. They had about three penny dolls each and their great delight was to dress and undress them. At present Dickie was saving up his sixpence a month to buy Nell a birthday book. He only needed one more sixpence and he could buy it.

After milking was over he went over to a shelf and look down a tin of marbles. How carefully he had hoarded those marbles up. His father had promised him a shilling (a rare event) if he could win 100 marbles in a week. With those he had had to give back, he would have had 112, and now—now today was Friday—and he had only 96. But he brightened up when he thought of the morrow. Saturday. Saturday was always a holiday from school, and where is the boy who has not brightened up at thought of a holiday.

"Dickie," said Mrs Sharpe from across the table. "Your father says you must go to old Mr Parrot's tomorrow with a message. You can stay there and play if you like."

"All right," said Dickie. He was thinking perhaps he might meet Mr James or Mr William, the event of which would give him the utmost pleasure. As he sat there he thought that he'd even be pleased to meet both.

Chapter 3

"I milked the cow last night, Jim, you'll have to milk her this morning."

The reader will easily guess who the speaker is. It is our young friend William Albert Parrot and he is (per usual), quarrelling with his brother James, on the chief worry of his young life—namely, the cow. How Master William and Master James used to bullyrag that cow. When, in blissful ignorance, she would hold her milk, what a time they would give her. How they would kick and punch her; she did it on purpose to aggravate them, of course she did. How many names they would shower upon her as she unconsciously chewed her cud while shut in the bail. And lastly, how they would brag to their old grandpapa of their prowess in milking such a hard cow.

Many an old farmer, on a visit to the old gentleman, would go off when he heard the boys talk, muttering as he did so, "Bad eggs, both of 'em, they'll come to no good".

But many of the greatest men of the times have had that same remark passed on them in their youth. However, James was at length bribed to milk the cow, and when he had pocketed William's penknife, he bailed her up and commenced. When, just half through he because aware of an onlooker. No less a young gentleman than Richard Sharpe. This was an embarrassing moment for James.

"Well," said Dicky, slowly.

James didn't answer but, darting off towards the barn, he reached the ladder, climbed into the loft, and promptly shut down the trap through which he had ascended, and sat on it. He then looked out of a small window and was surprised to see that Dicky, instead of chasing him, had turned on his heel and walked over in the direction of the house.

"He's scared of me, the coward!" said James Marmaduke, carefully lifting up the trapdoor, and descending boldly.

A brave lad was James. His former flight had been made without thinking, just on the spur of the moment. Meanwhile, Dicky Sharpe proceeded to the house, gave his note to Mr Parrot, and returned to the shed again. But the bird had flown—James Marmaduke was gone. So Dicky, after lingering about for some time in the hope that he would return to the half- milked cow, returned home.

Dicky was not of a revengeful nature. He hated a quarrel and was never known to pick one with anybody. But he had fully determined to have it out with the brave James now the quarrel was picked. Yes, Richard knew that James had cheated and lied about him, had caused him to be disgraced at school, and had got him a thrashing—not to mention the loss of the shilling which his father had promised him if he won 100 marbles. Let him quarrel; if he had the pluck to stand up to a boy half a head taller than himself, why, let him. He was in the right, no matter how you twist and turn the case.

Dicky returned home and spent the rest of the day with George Buston, a firm friend of his.

Meanwhile, our brave heroes, James and William, after finishing the cow returned up to the loft to discuss matters. They came to a very wise conclusion. Both agreed that to keep together was the main object for personal safety, as the little coward wouldn't—they were sure—attack both of them at the same time. Having agreed upon these matters the two boys went inside, and found their grandpapa at his desk.

Now, old Mr Parrot (though utterly devoid of spirit in most things) was an ardent naturalist and collector of such specimens as birds' eggs, butterflies, moths, and other such. Many an unsuspicious moth reposed in his desk; many a bright-winged butterfly lay pinned to his pieces of cardboard; and many were the rows of birds' eggs that his desk boasted. It was the old gentleman's hobby, and it afforded the two boys amusement, for they were always taken out on a collecting expedition, because an old man of 70 could not be reasonably expected to climb a tree whenever he located a bird's nest. As I have said, the boys found their grandpapa at his desk.

"Boys," said he. "I'm going out to find some nests, so you can come too."

The boys, though loath to go, were compelled to, and the old man led the way to a small bush not far from the house. He, after some time, found a nest, and sent William Albert up to get the eggs. But the young gentlemen couldn't climb that sort of tree. Upon a little persuasion, however, he attempted to climb up and, when he got to the top, admitted that he couldn't see anything of the nest.

"More to your right!" shouted Grandpa.

"Here," said William. "Is it here?"

"No, a little lower."

William very carefully descended at this, putting his foot into the hidden nest and smashing all the eggs as he did so. After this catastrophe, more bird's nesting was out of the question, so they went home again.

How poor, simple old men are sometimes imposed upon by their mischievous grandsons. What many a grandson wants is, I fancy, a touch-up with a switch.

Chapter 4

At four o'clock on Monday morning, Dicky Sharpe was up and in the cowshed. How he milked. Dicky was looking forward to school time and he was in a hurry. Of course I don't mean to imply that Master Richard was fond of going to school; he was merely thinking of how James Marmaduke Parrot would look when he had placed him hors de combat—that is, (out of action. Dicky bolted his breakfast, grabbed his luncheon kit, and sailed off to school, a full half an hour before his time. He was soon surrounded by a crowd of sympathising friends who tried to get him to have a game of marbles, but Dicky was determined.

"No," he said. "I got into a row on Friday through playing and I shan't have another game till I've settled Mr Jim."

That day, when our two friends, James and William, appeared at school they were received with hisses and cries of "Sneak!" and "Liar!" This was very discouraging, certainly, and both boys were glad when school went in. At dinner hour, as the boys still continued nastily, James made them a little speech.

"Now, you chaps," said he. "I'll just tell the teacher if you don't stop and leave us alone. He'll soon stop your cheek."

This speech was received with a hiss, and numerous were the names volleyed at the two. One boy went up, hat in hand, and requested Sir Marmaduke just to subscribe a few marbles for the benefit of a poor bankrupt fella, who'd been cheated out of his. The charitable collector came away from his peer with a look of disgust on his face.

"The old skinflint wouldn't give a marble," he said solemnly.

Such were the jokes constantly placed on the brothers, who began to seriously repent of ever having anything to do with Dicky and his marbles. But Dicky hadn't done with them yet, quite. After school was over James and William went off home before he could say a word to them, and the old school teacher proceeded to his house in very thoughtful state of mind. If the truth were known he was thinking of whether he had not punished Dicky unjustly. Everything told for the boy's innocence. His conduct. The conduct of William and James, and the conduct of all the other schoolboys. Boys seldom side with a cheat when there is a row on, as we know.

For a whole week this state of affairs continued, and our two noble friends led a miserable life. How eagerly they looked forward to Saturday. Their great names even were a hindrance to them, and many a time did the stately James Marmaduke Parrot wish his name were just plain Tom Parrot, or Ned Parrot.

Saturday they could be found (together of course) milking the cow. As their conversation was by no means pleasant, and was altogether of a doleful character, we will go over to where Dicky was cleaning out his shed, at home. Dicky's thoughts were also doleful. He was thinking of his repeated failures in meeting James face to face.

When the shed was finished he went inside and was accosted by Mrs Sharpe, who held a letter in her hand.

"Dicky," said she. "Your uncle, Ben, is coming to visit us here. How will you like that?"

Dicky frowned. "I suppose I'll have to keep half smothered in good clothes," said he.

"I don't think so. Your uncle isn't very particular about good clothes," said Mrs Sharpe, with a smile.

"I hope not," sighed Dicky. "When does he come?"

"He leaves home next week, so he'll be here in eight days," said Mrs Sharpe, referring to the letter. "Now mind, Dicky, you're not to say 'dash' or 'hang it' while he's here.

"All right," answered Dicky, "I'll be very careful."

"That's right," said his mother. "Nell! Tillie! Come here."

The two girls came running up and were forthwith given a little motherly advice as to what they were to do, and what they were *not* to do, when Uncle Benjamin came. Just at the end of these little advices, Mr Sharpe came in and announced to his wife that he was going to drive to Hāwera, and Dicky would have to accompany him. Dicky was delighted, to be sure, and he was soon ready. He took the money he had saved up with him, for he thought it not at all unlikely that his father might give him a sixpence, in which case he could buy little Nell's birthday book. Mr Sharpe did give his son sixpence, so Dicky bought a small red-covered book with his money, and retired from the shop, highly pleased, with the book wrapped in paper under his arm. Master Richard is not the only boy who thinks that to spend a few shillings is a great affair.

When Dicky got home and presented his book to little Nell, of course there was a great to-do, and he was the hero of the hour. Even his father condescended to smile on him, and actually sprung another sixpence, which he was to spend on himself.

We will now return to the Parrot household. James and William, having milked the cow, went to the loft, and, after they had carefully placed a log over the door, took off their coats and rolled up their sleeves. These were strange preparations, as the reader will probably observe. And, on the low rafter of the loft there hung a feather pillow. A feather pillow. It swung on a short rope, and was very dirty and dusty looking. The reader has probably seen these punching bags, which are used for training boxers. Well, that is what this pillow is supposed to represent. A pig's bladder was tried first, but it once— while the brave James was operating on it—bounced back and hit his face such a resounding whack that James absolutely refused to train himself any more.

Upon William smuggling the pillow up, he again fell to, however, and with such a good will that he soon had the pillow in the state I aforementioned. Nor was William behind hand in attacking the pillow, and, while James volleyed blows on one side, William returned them on the other.

"Now, look out!" said James, diving into the pillow.

"Here goes!" said William, doing ditto.

"Here goes again!" said James, making a terrific rush at the enemy again.

Unfortunately the enemy swung away at this moment, and James, instead of hitting the pillow, came a nerve-shaking bump, fist first into William, who had also at that moment made a dive.

The two brave heroes, when they had risen from the floor whereon the shock had sent them, began to nurse their heads and weep copiously. This little matter of form over, they proceeded over to the house, and were there met by Polly. This household domestic was in a very fluttered frame of mind.

"Oh, mister Willie," said she. "I can't find your pillow anywhere. I've looked under the bed, and out the window."

Willie burst into a hearty laugh which somewhat surprised poor Polly

"Whatever have you been doing with your eye?" she said, when she had gained her breath back. "It's quite black."

At this William Albert blushed, and walked off. When next Polly visited the boys' bedroom she found a soiled and dirty pillow in place of the clean one that James's bed had formerly boasted.

Chapter 5

Nothing worth relating occurred during the next week, except on Wednesday when James was kept in school. Of course William waited for him, and Richard, thinking he had a chance to avenge himself, ran down the road and hid behind a hedge the boys had to pass. They soon made their appearance, walking along carelessly, and Dicky got ready to jump from behind his cover.

James Marmaduke was just on the point of asking his brother a question when, with a "Houpha!" out sprang our young hero, Dicky, catching him by the neck and knocking him over. 'Alas for enterprise' as the great writer would say. Richard had counted on William Albert running off and leaving his brother to the fates. To the honour of that young gentleman, however, he did not run off, but quickly sprang to James's aid and, while he held Dicky down, James sat in the post of honour on the fallen enemy's head. In vain Richard struggled. He was firmly held, and he had time to seriously regret ever being so rash as to attack both the boys at once.

When he was at length allowed, by his triumphant conquerors, to rise from his ignominious position, he ran off home without a word, while James and William, highly elated, hurried off to bore Grandpapa with a complicated account of the occurrence. This sad failure of Richard's plans only made him the more determined to do something to square up, but no chance came to him for some time.

Not long after this, Grandpa Parrot had to drive to the station for some boxes, so he took his two grandsons with him. When the train pulled up at the station, a pleasant, broad-shouldered man of about

35 years stepped out, and, as he was going in Grandpa's direction, that old man asked him if he would like a ride. The stranger replied in the affirmative and, after handing up a portmanteau, he jumped in. The usual weather remarks were passed and then the stranger, turning to the boys, asked them if they knew little Dicky Sharpe. The boys acquiesced in a painful manner, and inwardly condemned their poor old grandpapa as a fool for letting such a man ride in the cart.

But their embarrassments were not yet over. The stranger wanted to know whether the boy was of a quarrelsome nature or not. Whether he was plucky, whether he had many fights, and lastly, whether he kept on good terms with his mates.

As you may suppose, it somewhat taxed the ingenuity of our two friends to answer these questions with accuracy, and with satisfaction to the questioner, and I'm obliged to confess that the accuracy of the answers was not very strictly studied. However, the general idea the stranger got of Richard was favourable, and he reached Mrs Sharpe's house under the impression that he was going to meet a plucky, quarrelsome, but pleasant lad—to wit, Dicky.

"Dicky! Nell! Tilly! Come here. Here's Uncle Ben," said Mrs Sharpe.

The stranger was the Sharpe's celebrated Uncle Ben. Dicky, Nell, and Tilly hung back shyly from their uncle, but several oranges, apples, and lollies, which that person drew from his pockets, soon induced them to forget their shyness, and Dicky was soon in the midst of a tale wherein Spotty the calf and Jack the dog played prominent parts.

Tilly had all her dolls laid out on her uncle's knee, and Nell was trying, amidst the clamour, to show him her birthday book.

"I saw two friends of yours today, Dicky," said Uncle Ben.

"Who were they?" inquired Dicky eagerly.

"I think they said their names were James and William Parrot."

Dicky blushed and frowned. "Where did you see them, Uncle?" he said.

"Oh, I rode from the station in their cart," he said. "What's this, Nell? Want me to see your birthday book, hey? Dicky bought it, did he? Why, there's hardly any other writing but your own in it."

Nell explained the reason. She wasn't going to have her book spoiled. When she asked anyone to write their birthday they usually said "Right, Nelly", dipped the pen to the bottom of the inkwell, dropped blots all over the page, and finally wrote their name in the wrong place and had to erase it out, and write it again. Uncle Ben laughed at Nell's reason for doing the writing herself, and they all went in to dinner.

Mr Benjamin Allan, brother of Mrs Sharpe, was a plain, good-humoured, and genial man, respected, as the book says, by friends and foes alike. At dinner he made no idle pretentions of a small appetite; he simply stated that he was as hungry as a horse, and fell to, evidently with great gusto. When he had furiously attacked his second plateful, he suddenly remembered that he had a present for each of the children.

He ridded himself of these little offerings with a hangdog air, and in his modest confusion, emptied the contents of his tobacco pouch into his teacup. Everybody at that moment appeared greatly absorbed in looking at the presents, however, so it was not noticed, and before they again looked up, Mr Allan had scooped the tobacco out of his cup with a teaspoon, and had deposited it under the table, onto the floor.

Dicky's present was a catapult or, as he called it, a shang-hai, with which to shoot stones out of, and many a good time did he afterwards have with it. Nell and Tilly each hugged small, waxen dolls, which, as their others were cheap china things, were greatly prized, and created quite a sensation in the doll corner of the house. Dinner over, Richard departed to a small bush to try his prowess with the shang-hai. He had barely got a supply of stones and reached the bush, when he heard voices.

Looking up he saw James and William Parrot quickly approaching him. Dicky's heart thrilled within himself and, quickly concealing the shang-hai, he shimmied up a nice, large branching tree, to the immense delight of our two heroes, who came along whistling cheerfully.

After lounging about for a couple of minutes at the foot of the tree, our two noble friends gave vent to some very ignoble sarcasms, and inquired of Dicky why didn't he come down. Dicky retorted, asking why didn't they come up. James and William said that was precisely what they meant to do, and they accordingly, each armed with a short switch, clambered up the tree, one on each side.

For a while they climbed steadily. Dicky watched their ascent with a calculating eye, and sawed harder at a thin branch he was trying to sever with his pocketknife. When they were nearly opposite him, he brought his waddy into play. Instantly the air was filled with screams and howls. James and William ordered a retreat without honour, while, amidst the cackle of the bending switch, and the laughs of Richard, the enemy followed.

In a flutter of excitement Dicky chased them to the ground where they at once turned at bay, so he again ascended the tree. Only for a yard or two, however, and, getting in a suitable position, he plied them so well with stones from his catapult that they turned and fled, with their hands to their ears.

At this ridiculous scene Richard laughed outright and, without giving them any more notice, he dismounted from his perch and returned home.

Chapter 6

James Marmaduke and William Albert cannot be reasonably expected to lie still without action after such a disgraceful check in their well-laid plans as they had experienced. They were, as I have before hinted, of a resourceful and clever nature, and the introduction of a catapult into their war affairs did not much discourage them.

So, if we visited their stronghold, the loft, we should see some very ingenious little arrangements. There was James, more earnestly at work than we have yet beheld him, with a needle and thread, some of Mary the housemaid's elastic, some old boots, and some small forked branches.

William was helping him and, in an hour's time, they managed to turn out a rather ingenious invention, which they persist in calling a shang-hai, though the relationship it bears to that formidable engine of destruction is so slight as to be absolutely unnoticeable. It suited the purpose, however, for which it was manufactured, and the two boys were simply charmed with the businesslike manner it lamed Grandpa's cat, when the works were set in motion. This contrivance was greatly prized by James and William and, in case Mary should remark on her elastic, it was hidden in the straw of the loft while not in use. When James and William had tired themselves out with practising with their shang-hai, they went inside, and were there made acquainted with the horrifying fact that they had to go over to Mr Sharpe's with a message.

They decided to make the best of things and, armed with the shang-hai and two short sticks, which they swung in a careless, dandified manner, they started off, alacrity in their manner, reluctance in their hearts. Dicky was in the garden when the boys reached their destination and, to reach the house, they had to go through a small wicket and along the garden path, just a yard or two from Richard.

"Hey," said James, sulkily. "Here's a note for your father."

No answer. Dicky appeared intent in weeding a small patch of onions.

"We can't wait all day," growled out William.

"I shan't wait on you, Mr James Marmaduke Parrot," said Dicky, suddenly rising. "If you've got a note, come in and give it to my father, not to me."

James and William very gingerly opened the gate and crept in. When halfway down the path Richard told them they'd better go back and shut the gate. At that moment they were within a dozen yards of Dicky, so William turned back with a run, followed by James, and together they shut the gate, and then they slowly crept back. Of course they weren't afraid. Of course not. But still they gave vent to two terrific breaths of relief when they had passed the stooping Richard, and found he wasn't going to attack them. Still, it was embarrassing.

Dicky also found it awkward and at last, unable to keep quiet any longer, he burst into a loud roar of laughter. A simultaneous roar at this moment came from the front room window, and there was Mr Benjamin Allan, his face red, and absolutely holding his sides with merriment. Seeing the boys' eyes directed to him, he doubled up, burst into a fit of coughing, and finally, with a purple face, emerged from the door and confronted the boys.

"Well," said he, biting his lip hard. "Come to play with Di—. Dick—. Ho! Ho! Ho! Ho! Ha! Ha! Ha!"

Here he was again seized by a fit of coughing, which evidently took some trouble to suppress, and it was a good two minutes before he spoke again. He apologised for his rude behaviour, saying he was somewhat subject to hysterics. Here another hysterical fit came on him, and the two boys, with scarlet faces, began to look somewhat uneasily around, as if they were on the lookout for a rescuer. They were not disappointed, for at that moment the door opened again, and Mrs Sharpe come out into the garden to see what was the matter. She inquired of Uncle Ben what was the matter.

"Oh! These little boys have come to p-play with Dick-kick-kicky..."

Here Uncle Ben was again seized with his ailment, namely hysterics and, when he again came to, he informed the boys with a solemn voice that he would have to visit Dr Lugglestop and see what that great man could do for him. At this Richard, who was behind his uncle, burst into a great laugh then was promptly stopped by a cuff on the ear, delivered by his mother with great gusto.

"I didn't—Ho! Ho!—I didn't know hysterics was catching," Uncle Ben was unkind enough to say. "Dicky, you might have to accompany me to the celebrated Doctor!"

By this time the boys were desperate and, pushing the note into Mrs Sharpe's hand, they turned and fled, followed by the sounds of two more hysterical fits, one of which was interspersed by a strange noise, not unlike a boy on the ear. When they got to the wicket they fumbled at the latch and, as is usually the case with hurrying people, they could not undo it. James hurled William away from it with such giant strength that he was only stopped by the intervention of a large cabbage, which was ruthlessly broken off for being in the way. William got up and took a terrified leap at the fence, landing on the top, and falling on his nose on the other side.

At that moment James got the gate open, and away they went, William with a nose not unlike a cherry, and James with a complicated mixture of elastic, leather and string trailing out from his pocket like the tail of a kite.

Chapter 7

Meanwhile, while the boys were thus retreating from the enemy, the enemy was in trouble. Mrs Sharpe and Uncle Ben both insisted on an explanation, and Dicky, much against his will, was forced to tell his story.

When Mrs Sharpe heard about the marbles she was naturally indignant, and when she heard that Dicky had been thrashed before the school, unjustly she was certain, she was wild, and pictured to herself a rather heated discourse with a certain old, stern-faced teacher whom she knew. Uncle Ben also was indignant and he vowed he'd prove Dicky in the right if he had to stay there a year. He also gave Richard half a crown for not being a telltale, and telling everyone.

Richard was pleased, and every five minutes he was seen fishing something out of his pocket and gazing intently at it. Gradually a smile would overspread his countenance, and he would slip the object of his delight back onto his pocket, and very carefully push a handkerchief down on top of it, so that it couldn't jolt out. A couple of days after this, while Richard was at school, a letter arrived from Mrs Allan, Mrs Sharpe's mother, inviting her to take a visit over to Wāitara and bring the two children with her. Mrs Sharpe accepted the invitation and, on Wednesday, off she went, accompanied by her two daughters.

Richard was too big for trips, and besides, he'd be wanted to milk the cows (although there was no necessity, as Uncle Ben was a good milker), and have the fire lit and the billy boiling. On the whole Dicky didn't mind being left behind. He thought baching would he good fun, and he looked forward to the thought of the indigestible pancakes he knew his father could make. Uncle Ben—also voted a considerable knowledge in affairs of the kitchen— and he, could make fritters, which one could digest with comparative safety. The rest of the week passed quietly and, on Saturday, Uncle Ben proclaimed his intention of taking Richard to town to spend his two shillings and sixpence.

After over an hour of patient working, he and Richard produced this little programme, which they both viewed with great satisfaction:

6 packets of crackers at 3*d*. = 1*s*. 6*d*.

3 bom-boms at 2*d*. each = 6*d*.

Other fireworks = 6*d*.

Total = 2*s*. 6*d*.

This little outlay, as the reader sees, is of a purely explosive character, and the bom-boms, large firecrackers, that make a terrific noise in exploding, were first thought of by Uncle Ben, who proposed with a wink and a frown, that it would be nice for one to explode a couple of inches off Mr James Marmaduke's ear. Dicky also thought it would be a pleasant scene, and he began to long for Monday.

Monday came, and with it came also the usual bustle and hurry of a school morning. James Marmaduke woke up and reached for his pantaloons. They were not there. He looked over to William, who was sleeping profoundly.

A thought crossed his mind. "Sleeping, are you," he muttered. "I'll soon wake you." He got up out of bed and gave James a severe buffet with a pillow.

"Come on," he said. "Give me my pants. I know you've hid them."

William woke up with a shriek, which speedily bought Grandpa, John, and Polly into the room. After a little trouble James's trousers were located, and hauled from under his bed, where he had probably kicked them while going to bed the night before.

That morning everything was wrong—the porridge was burnt, the tea smoked, the milk sour, and the bread stale. Also, James's dinner kit was missing from where it usually hung, and at last, in great bad humour, the boys got away to school.

At school the boys were unusually nice and friendly. They got James nicely on the talk, and they informed William that he was a fine plucky chap to stand up for his brother as he did. James's ill humour vanished, and he felt exultant at the good turn things had taken. In a communicative state of mind he began to describe how he and William had sat on Dicky, when . . .

Fiss! Bang! Pop!

James jumped up from the reclining posture he was in with a screech. All the boys around were laughing, and there, a yard from where he had lately sat, was Richard, with a shattered bom-bom in his hand. An exultant grin pervaded his features. A grin of real, downright maliciousness, which made James boil inwardly, and drove him to imprudence and desperation. He turned and ran into school. The teacher was near the window, and his usually grim and silent face was broken up by a smile of amusement. James began to doubt the wisdom of his course. He stated his case in a hesitating, scared manner, much to this effect:

"Er, please sir, er, please. Dicky Sharpe fired a b-big c-cracker at me."

"I think, James," said the teacher, smothering a smile. "I think if you would not tell so many tales, you'd get on much better with the other boys. Now be off, and don't let me hear any more about it."

James Marmaduke retired abashed. The one solitary hope remaining to him had been dashed to the ground. The teacher took no notice of his little informing game, and he was hopeless. As Mark Twain says: 'Life seemed hollow to him, and existence but a burden.' With depressed spirits he walked dejectedly out into the playground. But his troubles were barely commenced. James abhors crackers. Always did. Nasty, dangerous things. Mr Richard Sharpe had half-a-crown's worth of them. A good idea of his opinion concerning them is conveyed to the reader's mind in the one little word he occasionally gave vent to: "Gran!"

The other boys expressed similar sentiments and, as the crackers were equally distributed among them all, James and William—especially the former—very soon began to wish that all the firework factories in existence had blown up, say, a couple of months before.

For, as James reasoned, no new factories could possibly be built again in two months, and consequently, no more crackers could be made, and no torture like he was suffering would be the far-reaching result.

Half-a-crown's worth of crackers could not, however, last long among nearly twenty boys and, by the time school had gone in, all had been fired. All except a bom-bom that Dicky had stored away in the remote recesses of his breeches pocket. Nobody knew of it. Richard had no idea of letting anyone know of it either, for any knowledge any boy might receive on the subject would be speedily imparted to James and William, and Dicky's plan was to get them off their guard, before bringing his fireworks again into play. So far, so well.

James jumped at the idea of there being no more crackers. He jumped at it, and clung on, like a drowning man would cling at a straw, for James was very willing to believe there were no more crackers. The fact that he saw no more of them, and Dicky's behaviour, all bespoke of absence of the dreaded article, and he began to feel a little easier, and even went so far as to sit down. But there was a sad awakening for him. At afternoon school he watched with feverish impatience the slow hands of the clock as it ticked steadfastly on. Half past three at last. The school was released and the pupils filed noiselessly out the door. Once outside, however, their pent-up feelings exploded, and each and all gave vent to loud expressions of delight at their freedom. All except our two friends, who remained silent. James couldn't find his hat. A small boy informed him that it was under the school; so James stooped down to prove the truth of this statement. He had his head just nicely under the school when a cry of warning came from William.

"Look out, Jim!"

Before Jim could look out, Richard came around the corner and, after placing the bom-bom, which he carried, close to James, he retired to watch the results.

James was in agony. His head was under the school, where it had easily gone, but to withdraw it was another thing. There he lay, a beauteous spectacle—to Dicky—and his fright became so great that he at last burst into a roar, which almost drowned the bang of the bom-bom as it exploded harmlessly off. The cause of his scare being over, he speedily extracted his head from its uncomfortable position and, after putting a dusty hat, which Richard gave him, on his head, off he went away from school as hard as he could. The fact is, James saw the teacher not a chain away, and he was shaking as if he'd had a fit.

Dicky also saw him. He turned red, eyed a patch on the toe of his boot attentively, and at last, hearing no stern voice addressing him, he ventured to look up. His eye met the master's and he at once dropped it to its former position.

"I think it's time you were going home, Richard," was all the teacher said.

"Yessir," said Dicky, glad to be relieved from his state, which was embarrassing. "I'm just going, sir," he said, and off he went accordingly.

Chapter 8

On Tuesday morning Dicky was informed by his uncle that he would have to stay away from school. Dicky enquired if his father said he could.

"Oh, that's all right," said Uncle Ben.

So Dicky was content, and said no more. That day, about noon, Dicky, who was reading a *Buffalo Bill* in his room, heard his uncle's voice calling him. He ran out, and there was Uncle Ben, waiting for him at the kitchen fire.

"Your father's gone to town," he said.

"Has he?" answered Dicky, watching Mr Allan's coat-tails, which were dangerously close to the fire.

"Yes. So now I want to talk to you. I suppose you'd like to prove that you didn't cheat that young villain of a Parrot at marbles, wouldn't you?" he said. "Well, I've got a plan."

"What is it?" inquired Dicky, eagerly.

"Well, couldn't you and another chap accidently meet the two of them in that bush you and they pass through going to school?"

"We could, I suppose," said Richard. "But what good would that do?"

"Well," said Uncle Ben, reflectively, "when you had them safe—and I don't think they'd struggle—you could fish out a paper and pencil and make him sign what's on it. How's this?"

Mr Allan walked along to the table and picked a piece of paper up very carefully. On it was this:

I, James M Parrot do hereby say that I, and not Dicky Sharpe, cheated at marbles on September:21-1903, and I also confess that I told a deliberate falsehood in connection with the same affair.

Signed: _____

The above confession, as we see, is well-planned out (for Uncle Ben, at all events), and he sat for a considerable time composing it. This done, he at once called Richard, to see if it would do.

"Joff!" said Dicky perusing the document for the third time. "Gran! I'll get George Burton to help me make him sign it. When William sees two of us, he'll run, I bet, as I can easily manage one."

Next day, after school, Dicky and George, who had their plans laid out, ran off, apparently home, as hard as they could. James saw them.

"That mean coward of a Dick Sharpe is pretty scared of us now," said James scornfully, seeing them, "Look at him!"

"Yes," said William, "he's pretty scared. Come on!"

They hurried on, talking on various subjects, until they reached the brush. They were still talking when two boys jumped out from the cover of a Kōwhai tree and, with fierce shouts, seized the terror-stricken James by the collar and knocked him down. William, seeing that the odds were against him, streaked off with a marvellous speed, and soon left his pursuers (who, by the way, didn't chase him) far in his wake. Meantime, James, who lay under the weight of Richard's knee, was in a sorry plight.

"We'll let you go if you do what we want you to," said Richard.

"Yes! Let me get up and I'll do it," gasped James.

Dicky let him get up and, while James stood wincing, with George Burton's hand grasping his neck, he produced a piece of paper from his pocket and held it before James's eyes.

"Looks like a cheap advertisement, a bit," observed James dryly, at risk of consequences.

Dicky was justly indignant. He wanted revenge. "Let him go, George," he said taking off his coat. "Let him go and I'll punch him."

But no sooner did James feel the grip loosen on his neck than he upped heels and ran as hard as he could. He heard the two boys panting close behind him and doubled his exertions, but all to no use. He, while looking back to see how much he had gained in the race, ran slap into a tree, with a violence far from pleasant, and was caught. This time Dicky and George used threats; they were going to have it done, and mighty quick.

"Come sign it," said Richard, threateningly.

"Won't," said James, sulkily.

"You'd better," put in George. "Or we'll whack you."

"You'd better not whack me," said James.

"Oh! Won't we just! George get two nice switches ready," said James. "Now, give him a tap up. And again while I hold the paper in front of him."

"Well, give me the paper," said James, at last.

"Here," said Dicky. "Take it."

"Can't write without a pencil," growled James again.

"Well," said Richard, pleasantly. "Who said you couldn't?"

"Ain't I getting the pencil?" said Dicky. "Here, grab this pencil now, while I get my knife. The pencil point's a bit worn."

Dicky sharpened his pencil, broke the point again, did ditto, and then handed it to James, who was looking on in savage silence.

"What shall I do," growled he.

"Oh, just stick your name down," smiled Richard.

"Shan't," said James, suddenly, and in a frenzy of anger. "Think I'm going to get myself into a row? If you touch me I'll tell Grandpa. So there."

"Ho, Ho, Ho," said Dicky.

"Ho, Ho, Ho" said George. "Soon change your tune."

"So we will," said Dicky. "Come on, write—one, two, three."

James, threatened by two switches, seized the pencil, and frantically wrote his name. Then, scared as he thought of the consequences of his action, he endeavoured suddenly to pull his left hand (which George held) loose, and tear the paper up. But Richard was too quick for him. He frustrated the desperate James by pinning his arms to his sides. Seeing the chance was lost, James Marmaduke resigned himself to fate, and desisted from struggling. When let loose, however, he gave vent to some furious expressions of his rage; even before he was at a respectful distance from them. This outburst, however, had no effect on the two friends, unless it was to evoke laughter, which pealed forth plentifully, and mercilessly.

James crept home miserably, his heart full of woe. Now he wondered what the blissfully unconscious William would say when he heard the tidings. Next he would wonder what the teacher would say when the truth was broken to him. And worst, but not least, he would wonder what the teacher would *do*.

These fearful thoughts weighed like nightmares on the terror-stricken James's mind. He began to brood over them. His usually fluent, though harsh, tongue was replaced by a moody and silent one, which William thought even more disagreeable than violent tantrums would have been. To questions he would answer with a snap; sometimes he would answer not at all, or only to say "Shut up" or some other equally polite answer.

This may have eased his mind, but William Albert could not bring himself to be content with such answers. They were not satisfactory and, to say the least, they were not polite. There are times when even the quietest of person's self-restraint gives way, and he announced his feelings and innermost thoughts to the world generally, and to private individuals directly.

When James informed William of what had happened, that young gentleman's anger broke all bounds and he became, for a time, a raging demon. He denounced James as a coward, as a cheat, as a wretch. He wanted to know why he signed it? Anger choked his utterances, and he was able only to show his anger and disdain by the fiery look in his eyes. He stuttered and danced from foot to foot, such was the height of his rage. When he, at length, cooled down, it was only to ask the miserable and dejected James whether he was going to bring William into the row, or leave him out.

Chapter 9

Seated in Mr Sharpe's parlour were two individuals: Mr Benjamin Allan, and Master Richard Sharpe. The latter was busy describing the events aforementioned, and his tale was sometimes—often, in fact—broken by a loud guffaw from the excited and enthusiastic listener. Dicky carefully hauled out a dirty scrap of paper from his pocket and handed it to his excellent uncle. Here it is:

I, James M Parrot do hereby say that I, and not Dicky Sharpe, cheated at marbles on September:21-1903, and I also confess that I told a deliberate falsehood in connection with the same affair.

Signed: James, M. Parrot.

The signature was written in a tremulous, shaky manner, which brought forth comments from the pitiless Uncle Ben, and caused an endless amount of laughter and derision.

The next day, at half past eight, Mr Dicky was at school. He was anxious. Five minutes before school, two very *un*anxious young gentlemen might have been seen slouching along to school. William and James, or rather—putting them according to their consequence and appearance in the world, and in society—James and William, are going to school, and, they firmly believe, to misery and whackings. The school bell rang. They crept into line, with eyes averted and heads down. James, lifting his eyes, met the old school master's stern ones and, dropping them, he caught sight of a curious young gentleman, and then another, and then another, all looking askance at him.

"Turn." The sharp voice of the master interrupted the silence. "Forward into school."

The long row of boys and girls filed steadily into school. Richard Sharpe, and James and William Parrot, stood out in the front. The three boys mentioned did as required. The old master retired a step, clasped his hands behind his back, and gazed steadily at the three in turn. At that moment, to be home, James would have forfeited all his worldly belongings. Gazing intently at the toes of his boots, he could not see the master, but his instinct told him he was being carefully examined.

"James!" said the teacher suddenly.

"Yes sir," muttered James, without looking up.

"Is this true?" sternly inquired the master, holding up a dirty scrap of paper. "Did you sign this?"

"Please sir, he and George Burton made me," said James, beginning to whimper.

"Made you? Made you, did you say?" inquired the master, scornfully. "Who made you?"

"Dick Sharpe and George Burton," whimpered James, now thoroughly scared. "Please, sir, they said they'd hit me if I didn't."

"Didn't what?"

"Didn't sign it, sir."

"Well, is it true? Come tell the truth now, is it true?"

James hung his head but was silent.

"James!" said the teacher, accompanied by a terrific rap on the desk with a cane. "If you don't answer my question I shall be obliged to thrash you, my boy. Come, is it true or not? Did you act basely as I am led to believe by this paper? Answer!"

This too was accompanied by another terrific rap.

"Please sir I—" stammered James, feebly.

"Yes or No!" roared the teacher.

"Y-yes," said James.

"Yes? Did you say? You did act so basely? You hear, James? Answer me."

"Yes, sir," whispered James, again.

"Then I think, sir, what you want is a through thrashing. However, I'll leave your sentence for Dicky here, and do what he says."

Dicky at once said he didn't care if James was let off, so after a severe lecture, James and William apologised to Dicky, and the disagreeable meeting adjourned. Dicky at once made friends with his two crestfallen enemies, and did all he could to show he bore no malice. At play hour he made a particular duty of playing with them, and the other boys, following his example, did the same. In a few days they were on the same footing with the boys as they had formerly been and, as the apples at this time began to ripen, they soon had several very warm friends, for all knew the Parrot's orchard, and many of the boys had no orchards at their place.

James and William, however, cared not for warm friends. They carried on much the same as usual, only, however, both thought it just as well to keep on good terms with Richard, and both agreed that the wisest thing would be to give him plenty of fruit. In this they were not mistaken. Though Dicky did not love the givers, he nevertheless loved the fruit, and he, in time, even began to look upon the givers with approval.

Pears, peaches, and apples fell to his lot, and he was at times so loaded that he took whole pocketfuls home to his sister, who had returned, and to Uncle Ben, who was still living at Mr Sharpe's.

Uncle Ben was to return home in a couple of weeks; he proposed to take Richard with him, but that was out of the question. Didn't Dicky milk 10 or 12 cows, night and morning? How could they get on without him? Who'd milk his cows? The problem was, if not solved, got over, and it was agreed that Dicky should go in the winter when the cows were dry. Uncle Ben was going to teach Richard to be a carpenter.

Richard had no objection. He thought carpentering good fun. He had once made a beautiful milking stool. He told his uncle of this, but he forget to mention that when he sat on it to milk a cow, the legs gave way and he was precipitated rather neatly over on his back. Of course to have told that would have spoilt the effect of the story.

One fine Saturday morning, a party of 20 persons started out on a trip to the beach. Four of them were horse-men; the rest—men, women and children—were in two large wagons. Among the contents of one wagon was the Sharpe family, and the two Parrot boys. All awkward self-restraint was thrown off, and the boys were determined to enjoy themselves. It was a Christmas beach party, and all were out for a thorough day. Many had towels, and all had luncheon kits and baskets.

The sky was azure, the sun beat down warmly, and not a breath of air disturbed the tranquillity of the bright and sunny morning. In one wagon, Uncle Ben could be seen. He was on his best behaviour and was keeping all the passengers roaring with laughter at his banter. The old school master was also there, in convulsions at something funny Mr Allan said, and all around had smiling faces. To fully describe the picnic would be to fill a book. I shall not attempt a description. Suffice it, they all enjoyed themselves immensely. Some walked bare- footed up and down the burning sands. Others again ran about collecting driftwood to boil the billy. By far the most went in bathing. Of the better were Dicky, George Burton, and James and William. What matter if James only went in up to his knees, and William little further.

They enjoyed themselves, and ate tremendous piles of sandwiches and cake when suppertime came round. At 4 p.m. the party started for home. Merry, sunburnt, and tired.

Dicky felt uncomfortable—George, James, and William had thoughtfully filled his knickerbockers with not-too-dry sand, and it was not all shaken out. James's face was as red as a turkey's. William was losing his face, gradually, but surely. The fact was, it was peeling off in layers, and looked not unlike a match striker. Uncle Ben, still funny, wanted to drive, as he said the former driver looked too sun-burnt to do that important duty. Uncle Ben's face put one in mind of an underdone roast.

When the wagons got home, however, the fun melted like butter on a stove. Most of the merrymakers looked ruefully on at the ten or twelve cows they were impelled to milk. Some of the ladies looked ruefully on their sunburnt faces and some, I believe, even went to the trouble of rubbing their countenances with cream.

The two Parrot boys got home in a collapsing condition, and when they had refreshed themselves by various good things, they felt well enough to quarrel about the cow. The dispute ended by James sally-ing forth with the pail, and William staying inside and cleaning some knives. Old Mr Parrot had interfered. He told them calmly but firmly that they would have to stop quarrelling or he would get four cows. Two each for them, night and morning. Needless to say, after that, the Parrot house was quieter and more peaceful than it had been for three or four long years.

And now, a while after the beach party, great preparations could be seen going on in the Sharpes' house.

Mrs Sharpe was leaning over a great steaming pot. Dicky was splitting firewood, as if his life depended upon it. Mrs Sharpe was plucking a great fat goose, and Uncle Ben was flying around with a tremendous noise, and no visible results. Only one with half an eye could see that these are the preparations every family goes through just before 25th December.

As Mr Allan observes, 'Christmas comes but once a year'. And why shouldn't it be a merry Christmas when it does come?

The steaming pot occupying so much of Mrs Sharpe's attention had in it, of course, the plum duff. The wood Richard so diligently chopped is, of course, for cooking purposes. And the goose taking all the merriment out of the merry Mrs Sharpe is, most certainly, the Christmas goose.

If turkeys are scarce to honest country folk, geese are not, and a good fat goose is as much relished by them as the choicest turkey. Indeed, few kings make so genuinely merry over the best turkey and wine of the land, as the Sharpes make merry over their homely goose and their common, home-brewed ale.

Christmas is merry time. Christmas is celebrated by a gorgeous feast, and a general shout of "hang up your stocking" by all the juvenile population of the land. Few bush settlements or townships but have not each their bush party, their beach party, or their river party, and if they don't have them exactly on Christmas Day, they have them on Boxing Day, so where's the odds?

As I have said, the Sharpe family were anticipating Christmas. James and William, and Old Mr Parrot, were to go over, according to promise, and help to vanquish the valiant plum duff and the formidable goose that were creating such a stir in the Sharpes' house.

Accordingly, Christmas morning, the two boys hurried over to have some fun before dinnertime. Old Mr Parrot was to make his appearance among the party at about 11 a.m. It may seem the three boys were rather too friendly with each other, but the truth was, Mr Allan was determined to have them so, now the trouble of the marbles was cleaned up. To this extent he had them frequently together, and his kindly intentions were not wholly a failure.

Dicky, now his honour was not under a cloud, felt that compassionate, grudging feeling all victors have to vanquish, and the two Parrot boys were friends, merely because it paid them to be so, and because their motto was: 'Discretion is often the better part of valour'. As I have said, the boys retired merrily to Mrs Sharpe's house. Their thoughts were chiefly of the delicious plum duff and fizzling goose they knew were there, and their eyes were turned impatiently on the Sharpes' house; just far enough off to look a delectable place full of hidden pleasures and excitements.

They reached the place at last and were duly surrounded by two small girls and one small (though *he* didn't think so) boy. Heedless of the two poor lads' confusion and dismay, the little girls crowded around them, intent upon making them kiss two new-looking dolls, which they had got as presents. They escaped at last, and were then introduced to Richard's presents: a knife with four blades from Uncle Ben, and a set of cricket things from his parents.

Dinnertime came round at last, and with it came Grandpapa. A merry party they all were, as they sat at the table waiting to be served. Mr Allan, as usual, took the lead in all matters concerning wit and fun. He was coolly asking could William spell 'cat' when that young gentleman retorted innocently, to the great delight of all the diners, that no, he couldn't spell 'cat' but he could spell 'donkey'!

"One for you, old chap!" said Mrs Sharpe, giving Mr Allan a slap on the back and laughing heartily while even Grandpa smiled. "Well done, young'un!"

"Ho! Ho!" laughed the merry Uncle Ben, disconcerted at this shot at his mental powers. "Ho, Ho, Ho—no fooling with you. Hey, you speak your mind out plain!"

"Don't blame him," said Mrs Sharpe. Nothing like a plain tongue. Some more sauce for your pudding, James?"

"He's saucy enough," growled Mr Allan, trying to smile, without letting anyone see him, and only half succeeding.

"Benjamin!" said Mrs Sharpe, severely. "Don't be rude."

"Beg pardon," said Mr Benjamin, solemnly, but winking villainously with the eye turned away from his corrector. "Awful sorry."

To show that his sincerity was real and not feigned, Mr Allan distorted his face, on the off-side from Mrs Sharpe, into a perfect volley of winks, frightful to behold. The only effect they produced on the merry company, however, was to evoke a storm of laughter, and so surprised was Uncle Ben at the noise his sorrow had caused, that he looked up quite astonished.

"What's the matter?" he ventured to ask.

This question caused more laughter, in the midst of which Richard took a mouthful of much too hot goose. Instead of trying to swallow it, that young barbarian calmly opened his mouth and dropped it onto his plate again.

"Many a fool would have swallowed that," he said, complacently.

After dinner was partaken of, the children had a game of Snapdragon. This consisted of a plateful of raisins and almonds well-saturated with some kind of spirits. When the game started, the spirits were ignited, and burnt a blue light all around the raisins. The players then had to snatch the fruit out of the flames. The bolder one was, the more he or she got. It was a case of 'none but the brave deserve the fare'. James and William each got enough for themselves, and Richard got enough for himself and his two sisters.

The next thing to be done was to have a game. Accordingly, a game of rounders was indulged in, Richard's cricket things being used in lieu of a rounders set. Sides were picked, and for a time the game proceeded merrily. Only one incident worthy of notice occurred. Uncle Ben, in the midst of an elaborate joke, felt a sudden stopper to his fun. The stopper came in the form of a ball, and nearly knocked his false teeth down his throat. About half an hour after this catastrophe, Uncle Ben, to the surprise of all, began to laugh heartily.

Though so clever at jokes usually, this one only struck him as funny half an hour after it had occurred. When it first struck him it felt anything but funny. In fact, as he afterwards said, it rather hurt. About four o'clock the Parrot trio returned to their dull old home, where the boys indulged in grim remarks at the expense of John, and the old man indulged in something else, that had came a day ago in a case. Labelled 'Pale Ale'.

Ten o'clock that night a thin, wheezy voice might have been heard issuing from Parrot's parlour window and singing, "Oh, what, is, the, matter with ME?"

And now, as near as the space will permit, I will finish my story.

James and William both lived with their grandpa for several years, until, reaching the ripe age of 18, they left their sheltering home and went out to do battle against the world. How they succeeded is not very well known, but James got into a business firm, and became so tangled up, that it was only his grandpapa's death that saved him from bankruptcy.

William became a farm labourer, but with his grandpapa dying he was able, with the money left him, to settle down and marry.

Richard accompanied his Uncle Ben to Hāwera, where he was duly taught the art of carpentry, and he in time became a great adept, and more skilful, even, than his teacher. He continued making doll's cradles and beds for his two sisters, long after they were too old to use such things, and he even built his mother a large meat safe, with drawers and shelves, all complete. He eventually became a great carpenter, and even had three men all under him, to help carry out his orders.

Richard's sisters both became great dressmakers, and accustomed to mix in high society. Tilly married a young Officer of the Law and is now Mrs Bennet, and Nellie is still single, though she has great expectations in the form of a young doctor, Mr Graham.

Mr Sharpe, at length, gave up milking, and he is now living on an annuity, forwarded to him by his successful son, Richard.

The End